...HORSE NAMED DRAGON

created by
GERTRUDE CHANDLER WARNER

Illustrated by Robert Papp

ALBERT WHITMAN & Company
Albert Whitman & Company

A Horse Named Dragon
Created by Gertrude Chandler Warner;
Illustrated by Robert Papp.

ISBN: 978-0-8075-5571-2 (hardcover)
ISBN: 978-0-8075-5572-9 (paperback)

Cover art by Robert Papp.

For information about Albert Whitman & Company,
visit our web site at www.albertwhitman.com.

Contents

Contents

A HORSE NAMED DRAGON

CHAPTER 1

Dare to Dream

Six-year-old Benny Alden bolted awake in the middle of the night. Where was he? He sat straight up in bed. His heart drummed.

This wasn't his bed!

Far away, a horse whinnied. Benny breathed a deep sigh. Now he remembered. He was on vacation with his brother and sisters at the Dare to Dream Ranch. This was their first night sleeping in the bunkhouse. But—what woke him?

Benny slid out of bed, careful not to wake

his big brother Henry asleep in the top bunk. He tiptoed past his sisters. Twelve-year-old Jessie's arm flopped over the side of the top bunk. In the bunk below, ten-year-old Violet cuddled her stuffed panda. The girls did not stir as Benny tiptoed past.

At the window, Benny pulled aside the curtain and peered out. The sliver of moon gave off little light. Benny could barely see the large barn in the distance. Far away, the horse whinnied again. But Benny could not see any horses. He listened to the night sounds. Crickets chirruped. Soft winds creaked the rocking chairs on the bunkhouse porch.

Wait! Were those voices? Whispers? Benny listened hard. A sudden gust of wind rustled the trees. He didn't hear any more voices. Maybe what he'd heard was just the sound of the wind.

The horse whinnied a third time. Benny heard a faint clip-clop of hooves. A truck engine started up. He listened as the truck drove away. Then, silence.

Benny yawned, then yawned again. He'd

better get some sleep. Tomorrow was the Alden children's first full day working and playing at the Dare to Dream Ranch.

Fourteen-year-old Henry woke at dawn. He jumped down from his bunk and looked out the window. Far across the ranch, he saw cowboys on horseback. "Eeeeee-haaaa!" came their faint shouts. "Eeeeee-haaaa!"

Henry ran to the bunks. "Wake up," he said, gently shaking his sleeping brother and sisters. "The wranglers are bringing the horses in from the pasture."

The excited children quickly washed, then dressed in jeans and T-shirts. They put on cowboy hats to shade them from the sun and cowboy boots for riding horses. Then they ran to the corral. The corral was a circle as big as a schoolyard, with a rail fence all around. The children scrambled up and sat on the top rail to watch. Wranglers on horseback called out "Eeeeee-haaaa," as they shooed horses in.

A spirited black horse ran into the corral. It had a large white spot shaped like a dragon on its back. "Dragon!" yelled Jessie, clapping her hands. Her favorite horse looked up and shook its head.

The other children searched for their favorite horses. Their grandfather, James Alden, often brought them to the Dare to Dream Ranch to ride. He and the owner, Cookie Miller, were childhood friends. Cookie had taught the children how to ride, and the children practiced hard. Each time they came, they rode better and better.

When Cookie heard that Grandfather Alden was going away on business for a few days, she invited the children to stay at the ranch.

"You'll have to work, just like regular ranch hands," she told them. "But you'll also get to ride." The Alden children liked to work, and they *loved* to ride. "Yes!" they had said, at once.

A small white horse with black dots walked into the corral.

"Lots-o'-Dots," called Benny. The little horse looked up and snorted. It trotted over to Benny. "He remembers me!" Benny cried. Lots-o'-Dots had been brought to the ranch a month ago. Benny was the first guest to ride him. The horse nuzzled Benny's pocket. "You're looking for a treat, aren't you?" said Benny. "I'll bring you something from breakfast."

A powerful brown horse burst into the corral. Henry put his thumb and pinky in his mouth and blew out a short, shrill whistle. The horse whinnied and reared up on its hind legs, pawing the air. Then it pranced over.

"Hey, Lightning," said Henry, scratching the horse behind the ears. "How are you, boy?"

Violet waited and waited, searching for her horse. "Does anyone see Daisy?"

"The horses are still coming in," said Jessie. "Daisy will be here soon."

But Violet was afraid Daisy was gone. Daisy was one of Dare to Dream's "rescue horses." These were horses rescued from all over the country. Some had wandered away from their homes. They were found sick or hungry or injured. Cookie nursed them until they were well. Then she found good families to adopt them. A year ago, a Boy Scout troop had found Daisy wandering the hills of Montana. The gray horse was skinny from hunger and hurt by a bobcat's bites. The troop sent Daisy to the Dare to Dream Ranch. Last month, when Violet came to ride, Daisy's wounds had healed and she'd grown nice and plump.

Violet watched the horses filling the corral. Most were regular horses, the ones ridden by wranglers and guest riders. But a few, like Daisy, were rescue horses.

"I still don't see her," said Violet. "Maybe she's been adopted." She *did* hope Daisy found a family to love and care for her. But Violet wished she might ride the gentle gray horse *one* more time.

"There," cried Jessie, "there's Daisy." And coming into the corral, prancing as prettily as a princess, was Violet's very favorite horse. "Here, Daisy. Here, girl." Violet laughed as Daisy danced over.

Suddenly, a wrangler came riding fast around the barn. Her face looked grim under her red cowboy hat. Her horse

thundered past the corral as it raced toward the main house.

"Something's wrong," said Henry, jumping down from the fence. The other children followed, running full speed. By the time they reached the ranch house, the wrangler was on the front porch talking excitedly to Cookie.

"Gone," the young woman was saying. "We must call the police. Someone stole Honey and Bunny!"

CHAPTER 2

Horse Thieves!

The children sat on the corral fence as Cookie and the young woman talked to the policeman. "So," the policeman said, writing in his notebook, "you're the new head wrangler."

The young woman nodded. "My name's Alyssa. I've been riding here at the ranch since I was a little girl. Last month, when the head wrangler retired, I applied for the job. Cookie put me in charge of caring for the horses."

"And you're sure two of them were stolen?" the policeman asked.

"Where else *could* they be?" she asked, her voice shrill.

Cookie patted the young woman's shoulder. "Every morning, Alyssa brings horses from the pastures to the corral so we can check them over." Cookie pushed a wisp of white hair off her forehead. "Some horses need shots or ointments. Others need their hooves picked, or new shoes put on."

"And we put out oats," said Alyssa. "Honey and Bunny love their oats. They're usually the first ones into the corral. But not . . . but not today . . . " She sniffed and stared down at her boots.

The children felt sorry for Alyssa. The horses were her responsibility, and now two of them were missing. "Maybe," said Violet, "they jumped over the fence."

"It's too high," said Alyssa.

"Besides," said Cookie, "Honey and Bunny wouldn't even try to jump. They are a couple of sweet old mares who spend their days grazing and sleeping."

The policeman scratched the back of

his neck. "Well," he said, "I do recall reading about a ring of horse thieves working in the next county. But that was a few months back. I never heard of any horses stolen from around here. Has your ranch had trouble like this before?"

"No," said the two women.

The policeman flipped his notebook shut. "You should call around. Ask your neighbors to keep an eye out for your horses." He climbed into his car. "I'll spread the word when I have time." He drove away down the dusty road.

"I'll go check the pastures one more time," said Alyssa, riding off.

"And I need to get back to my kitchen before I burn up breakfast," said Cookie. "I'll ring the cowbell when it's time to come eat."

The four Alden children sat quietly on the fence, thinking. It was well known back home in Greenfield that the children loved to solve mysteries. But they never expected to find one at the Dare to Dream Ranch.

Finally, Jessie said, "Well, if you ask me,

this doesn't make any sense at all."

"What doesn't?" asked Violet.

Jessie turned to her sister. "Pretend you're a horse thief."

Violet gasped. "Oh, I would *never* steal—"

"Just *pretend*," said Jessie.

"*I'll* do it!" said Benny.

"Good," said Jessie, "you're the thief." Benny made a mean face. "Perfect. Now, here you come, sneaking around this ranch in the dead of night. You see a pasture filled with beautiful horses. You can steal any one of them. So, do you steal a couple of tired old mares?"

"Not me!" said Benny. "I'd steal Lots-o'-Dots, 'cause he's the best."

"And I'd steal the fastest and the strongest horses I could find," said Henry. "Like Lightning and Dragon."

"Exactly!" Jessie said. "That's why this doesn't make sense."

They sat quietly, thinking, watching the corral full of horses. The Aldens always felt a special bond with the rescue horses on the ranch. These children also knew how it felt to be homeless. After their parents died, they had run away and lived all by themselves. One stormy night, they found an old boxcar in the woods, and soon made it their home. They lived there until Grandfather found them and brought them to live with him. Like the rescue horses on Cookie's ranch, the children knew how hard it was to be on their own, and how wonderful it felt to find a safe and loving home.

"What's Dragon doing here?" boomed a deep voice. A big man rode up. He wore an old straw cowboy hat. His long blond moustache curled up at the ends.

"Dragon is my horse," said Jessie. "I'm going to ride—"

"He's not ready," the man snapped. "He cut his leg. Alyssa was told to keep him in out in the west pasture until it healed."

"Who are you?" asked Henry.

"Kurt Krupnik, the new ranch manager," the big man said. "Alyssa better learn to listen to me if she wants these horses to stay healthy.

I told Cookie that girl is too young to be head wrangler." Then he whirled his horse around and rode away.

"Do you really think something's wrong with Dragon?" asked Jessie. They watched Dragon walk around the corral. He didn't limp or seem hurt. Maybe Kurt was wrong. Maybe Dragon's leg *had* healed.

Clang, clang, clang. A loud cowbell rang. "Break-fast," called Cookie. *Clang, clang, clang.* "Come and get it."

The hungry children scrambled down from the fence and joined the ranch hands and volunteers heading toward the main house. Violet was nearly at the door when she realized Benny was missing. Something was wrong—Benny was *always* first in line for food! She ran back to the corral. Benny still sat on the fence, scratching Lots-o'-Dots behind the ear.

"Benny," she said, "you'll miss breakfast."

"I'm not going," he said.

"Why not?"

"If I leave, someone might come and steal

Lots-o'-Dots. The way they stole Honey and Bunny."

"Don't you worry." An old man limped up carrying two buckets filled with oats. He looked like Grandfather with his white hair and nice smile. But this man was a little shorter and a *lot* rounder. A ragged band of bright orange feathers decorated his cowboy hat. Some feathers were bent, and some were missing. "My name's Bucky," he said. "I volunteer here at the ranch. And I can guarantee that Lots-o'-Dots will be right here when you finish your breakfast."

"How do you know?" Benny asked.

"Well, now, if there's one thing Lots-o'-Dots likes, it's a handful of these oats." He held a bucket out to Benny. "If you feed him some, he'll wait around for you to come back."

Benny scooped a handful of oats and held them out. Lots-o'-Dots gobbled them down and snorted for more.

"Are you sure no one will steal him?" asked Benny. He didn't want to leave, but his

stomach was growling for breakfast.

"I'll keep an eye on him for you," said Bucky. "Now, you'd better hurry. Cookie serves the best flapjacks in the county."

"Flapjacks?" asked Benny.

"They're like pancakes, but a whole heap bigger. And Cookie serves 'em up with powdered sugar and hot maple syrup."

That did it! Benny jumped down from the fence and raced Violet all the way to the ranch house.

At the door, he stopped and looked back at the corral. Lots-o'-Dots poked his nose through the fence, waiting for Benny to come back.

The dining room rang with lively voices. There were wranglers who worked with the horses and volunteers who helped nurse the rescue horses. Cookie sat with the children at a long wooden table. A skinny man with thick black hair sat at the head of their table.

"This is Slim," said Cookie. "Our regular doc broke his leg and can't work for a couple of months. Slim here is filling in as the ranch's veterinarian."

"Wow, you're an animal doctor!" said Benny.

"Like the vet who takes care of Watch."

"Is Watch your horse?" asked Slim.

"Watch is our dog," Benny said. "Watch dog. Get it?"

Slim grunted. "I love dogs," he said. "Know all about 'em. Heck, I once wrote a book about how to raise dogs. It was called *How to Raise Dogs*. Yessir, next to horses, I like doctoring dogs the best."

Slim reached his arm across Benny for the syrup. Even though Slim's hair was black, the hair on his arm was red. "Soon as I settle in," Slim was saying, "I mean to get me a dog. Maybe two. Heck, maybe three." Benny stared at Slim's throat. A bump in the middle bounced up and down when he talked.

"Will you look at Dragon's leg after breakfast?" Jessie asked. "Kurt said I can't ride Dragon unless you say it's all right. Dragon is right out in the corral."

Slim frowned. "I told Alyssa to keep him out in the west pasture for a few more days. Until he heals."

"Please," Jessie begged. "He isn't limping or anything."

Slim leaned back in his chair, balancing on the back two legs. "I have a lot to do this morning. But I'll try to check him out later."

"Oh, thank you," said Jessie, crossing her fingers as hard as she could.

"Slim, here, is real good at finding rescue horses," said Cookie. "In the month since he moved here, he's brought in a whole bunch."

"That's because people all across these United States know I like to help horses in need," Slim said proudly. "I've been helping rescue horses for years."

Benny watched the bump in Slim's throat dancing up and down. Grandfather had a small bump in his throat. "It's called an Adam's apple," he'd said. "It's where the voice box is." But Grandfather's Adam's apple never danced like Slim's. Benny's mouth hung open. Henry tapped his foot against Benny's. Benny kept staring. Henry leaned over and whispered, "Stop staring." Benny tried. But he just couldn't help himself.

"There's Alyssa," said Cookie, waving. The wrangler's shoulders sagged as she walked across the dining room. She took off her red hat and sat next to Cookie. "I searched every one of our pastures," she said. "Honey and Bunny are gone."

Cookie picked up a spoon and clinked her water glass. The room grew quiet. She told everyone about the missing horses.

"Did any of you see or hear anything unusual last night?" she asked. Benny raised his hand.

"Yes, Benny?"

"I heard a horse whinny," he said. Everyone burst into laughter. Benny slid down in his chair, embarrassed.

"Thank you, Benny," said Cookie. "But here on the ranch, it would be strange *not* to hear horses whinny now and again." She looked around the room. "Did anyone else hear anything?"

Benny was going to tell them about hearing a truck start up in the middle of the night. But he was afraid they'd laugh at that,

too. So he just reached for the maple syrup
and poured it all over his second helping of
Cookie's famous flapjacks.

CHAPTER 3

No Dessert Until . . .

After breakfast, Cookie and Alyssa walked the children back to the corral to see their horses. Benny spotted Lots-o'-Dots standing with Bucky in a shady corner. "Here, boy," he called. Benny held out a biscuit he'd saved from breakfast. Lots-o'-Dots trotted over and gobbled it down.

Bucky limped over carrying the empty oat buckets. "I told you he'd be here," said Bucky. As Bucky climbed through the fence, his hat with the orange feathers fell off.

Lots-o'-Dots picked it up in his big horse teeth. Everyone laughed. Bucky grabbed it back, then glanced shyly at Cookie as he put it on. Cookie smiled, her eyes twinkling.

"Are we going to ride now?" Benny asked.

"Not yet," Cookie said. "When you live on a ranch, you have to do your chores first."

"We cowboys have a saying: 'No dessert until you finish your mashed potatoes,'" said Bucky.

"I *always* finish my mashed potatoes!" exclaimed Benny.

Cookie laughed. "What Bucky means is, we don't get treats—like riding our horses—until we finish our work."

"What can my job be?" Violet asked cheerfully.

"Your grandfather tells me you're a wonderful artist," said Cookie. "I'm putting you in charge of the barn project. That big barn over there faces the highway. Lots of people drive by every day. I'd like to paint a mural on the side."

"A mural?" asked Benny.

"A big painting on the side of a building, or on a wall," said Violet. "Like the dancing fruits and vegetables painted on the wall at Faber's Finer Foods."

"Right," said Cookie. "A nice big mural could show people that the Dare to Dream Ranch has horses to ride and horses to adopt."

Violet looked at the huge barn. "I . . . I don't think I can paint that all my myself."

"You just make the drawing," Cookie said. "Bucky here will round up our volunteers to do the painting."

Kurt Krupnik rode up. The ranch manager's blond moustache was as dusty as his horse.

"I think I know what happened to Honey and Bunny. A big tree branch fell on the fence in the far pasture," he said. "It tore down a whole section. Honey and Bunny probably saw the opening and just walked on out of here. I've sent a couple of my men to look for them. You never should have called the police, Alyssa."

"I . . . I thought the horses were stolen," Alyssa said.

"If you had more experience, you wouldn't panic." Kurt looked at the horses in the corral. "Why is Dragon still up here?" He glared at Alyssa. "He's supposed to be out in the west pasture, in the old corral."

Alyssa jutted her jaw. "I think his leg is healed."

"You're not the vet," Kurt said. "Dragon stays out in the old corral until Slim gives the okay."

"Let me take a look," said Bucky. He climbed into the corral and lifted Dragon's back leg.

Jessie stared at Dragon's shoe. Most horse-shoes were shaped like a "U" but Dragon's had a square toe. "What's wrong with his foot?" she asked

"Oh, that's nothing," said Bucky. "I noticed that Dragon here liked to 'wing it' when he ran. Kicked his leg up to the inside. This square-toe shoe helps him run nice and straight." He set Dragon's foot back down. "His leg looks healed," he said.

Kurt frowned at the white-haired man. "No one rides Dragon until the vet checks him out," he told Bucky.

"You're the boss," said Bucky. He grabbed hold of Dragon's bridle. "I'll put him in his stall until Slim can look at him."

"You'd better," Kurt grunted, riding off.

"Why is Kurt so angry?" asked Henry.

"He hates me," said Alyssa. "He thinks I'm too young to be the head wrangler. He wanted his best friend, a wrangler in Kentucky, to get the job."

"Now, now," said Cookie. "Kurt's just looking out for the horses. I swear, sometimes he's like a mother hen protecting her chicks."

*   *   *

Honk. Honk. A green van roared up to the corral and screeched to a stop. A woman jumped out. Her long hair flew crazily in all directions and her wrinkled clothes looked like she had slept in them. She waved a stack of purple flyers. "Have any of you seen my horse?" she asked, passing out flyers. They said:

STOLEN HORSE — REWARD

HAVE YOU SEEN BUTTERCUP?

There was a phone number and a photo of a beautiful gray horse with a white patch on its nose. Its tail was white and black. "Buttercup's been missing for two days," said the lady.

"Two of our horses are missing!" said Benny.

The woman gasped. "Were they stolen, too?"

"They may have walked out through a broken fence," said Henry.

Violet felt sorry for the lady, whose eyes were red from crying. "Maybe your horse wandered off, too," she said.

"No." The woman's eyes brimmed with tears. "Someone cut the lock on our gate.

Buttercup was definitely stolen. Your missing horses may have been stolen, too." Her hand trembled as she held up a flyer. "You should make flyers like this to pass out to people."

"I don't have photographs of my horses," Cookie said.

"Then you'd better take some," warned the woman as she climbed back in her van. "Right this very minute." And she drove away.

Jessie studied the flyer. "I brought my new birthday camera," she said. "I can take photos of all the horses on the ranch."

"Are you sure? It seems like an awful lot of work," Cookie said.

"I'll help," said Violet. She held up the flyer. "This picture shows people exactly what Buttercup looks like."

Bucky walked by, leading Dragon by the bridle. He nodded at the flyer. "Too bad we don't have photos like that of Honey and Bunny to show around." He winked at Cookie. "It's no use closing the barn door after the horses get out."

Cookie's cheeks blushed red. "Oh, all right,"

she said. "You girls best get started while the horses are still in the corral. Once we turn them out to pasture, they scatter every which way." The girls ran off to get Jessie's camera.

"What's my job?" Henry asked, eager to begin.

"Your grandfather told me you're handy with tools," said Cookie. "I want you to saddle up and go help Kurt mend that broken fence." Henry dashed off to saddle Lightning.

"What about me?" asked Benny.

"You'll water the horses," Cookie said. "That means filling water buckets, tanks, and barrels all around the ranch. Bucky has a map that shows where they are."

"Let me put Dragon in his stall," Bucky told Benny. "Then I'll get you started. Be right back."

Benny waited at the corral. He watched Henry throw a blanket over Lightning's back, then cinch on the saddle. "It's no fair," he grumbled, when Bucky came back. "Henry gets to ride and I don't."

"I'll tell you a secret," said Bucky. "Of

all the jobs on the ranch, yours is the most important."

"Really?" said Benny.

The old man pushed his hat back. "Benny, I've been a rancher over fifty years. And one thing I know is true is that horses can't live without plenty of fresh water. Each one of them drinks ten to twenty-five gallons of water a day." Benny pictured the big gallon milk bottle in his refrigerator back home. He tried to imagine drinking twenty-five of them. It made his stomach hurt just thinking about it.

"Besides," Bucky smiled, "watering the horses is the most fun job . . . and the coolest." He took a map out of his pocket. "Here—this is a map of the ranch." He pointed to a big circle in the middle. "Here's the corral, where we are now. And these," he pointed to small red Xes all around the map, "these are water containers that need filling."

"There's so many," sighed Benny. "I can't fill them all."

"Sure you can. The trick is to start with

the first one," Bucky ran his finger up the map to the farthest *X*, "then fill the next and the next. Just take them one by one. Before you know it, you'll be right back here in time for lunch."

Benny watched Henry climb up on Lightning and ride off across the pasture. "I really really really wish I could ride right now," said Benny.

"You'll be riding soon enough," said Bucky. "but, first . . . "

"I know, I know," said Benny, looking at all the *X*es on the map, "first I need to go finish my mashed potatoes."

CHAPTER 4

Tracking the Hoofprints

Henry raced Lightning across the ranch. He rode and rode until he saw the huge branch that had crushed the wire fence. "Whoa, boy," he said, pulling back on the reins. Henry climbed down and tied Lightning to a tree, then went to take a look. The heavy branch had pulled down two fence posts and snapped the fence wire. The ground was littered with small brown leaves and long brown pods from the tree branch.

A shiny new car drove up the road near

the broken fence. Slim the vet was driving, and he rolled down the window and waved to Henry. "What's all this?" Slim asked, his Adam's apple bobbing.

"The branch fell and broke the fence," said Henry.

Slim nodded. "So, that's where Honey and Bunny escaped. Good to know they weren't stolen. Well, I'm off to buy medicine for the horses. See you later."

Henry tried pulling the branch, but it was too big and heavy. Kurt drove up on a small tractor. In back were a big toolbox, rope, some fence wire, and a post digger.

"That branch must have blown down during the night," Kurt said. He picked up the rope and tossed one end to Henry. "Here, wrap this around the branch and I'll pull it off with the tractor."

Henry went to work winding the rope around and around the branch. Jagged bark scraped his arms, and branches scratched his face. Sharp twigs snagged his clothes. The long brown pods slipped underfoot. Henry worked hard, tying the rope good and tight.

"Ready," he said.

Whirrrrr, whirrrrr. The tractor strained, slowly pulling the branch away from the fence. Dead leaves and pods fell off.

"I'll take this over to the burning pit," Kurt said. "That's where we pile the brush that needs burning. When I come back, we'll fix this fence." And he drove off, dragging the branch away.

Henry patted Lightning as he leaned against the tree to wait for Kurt. Someone had carved a heart into the tree bark. Inside they'd carved *TA + LM*. The heart looked faded from many years of freezing winters and hot summers. There was a hole in the bark below the heart. No woodpecker made this hole. It was as big as Henry's finger, and perfectly round. Someone drilled this hole. But why?

He walked around the other side and found two more holes. A scrap of paper poked out

of one. Henry reached up and pulled it out. Someone had written: *Gray Arabian. Brown spotted pony.* Maybe this was the way ranch hands left messages for each other, Henry thought.

Lightning whinnied again. "Easy, now," said Henry, putting the paper back. When Kurt returned, Henry would ask about the note, and about the heart carved into the tree.

*   *   *

"Hold still!" cried Jessie.

"I'm trying." In the corral, Violet gripped the bridle of a white horse that kept pushing her with its nose.

Jessie pointed the camera, trying to take a picture. "He keeps moving."

"That's because he wants the whole apple." Violet reached into her pocket and took out another piece of cut-up apple. "Get ready," she said, holding the apple in her fist under the horse's nose.

Jessie aimed her camera until she could see the whole horse from its nose to its tail, and its ears to its hooves. "Ready!"

Violet slowly opened her fingers. "Now!"

Jessie clicked the camera as the horse gobbled the apple. "Got it!" said Jessie.

Cookie brought tall glasses of lemonade to the girls. "You're doing a fine job," she said.

"We're only half done," said Violet. "Dare to Dream has so many horses."

Cookie laughed. "This is nothing. When I was a little girl, we had a couple of hundred horses on this ranch. And we had cattle and chickens and I don't know what-all. My folks had lots of help back then. Whole families lived here. My best friend, Trevor, lived right in that bunkhouse where you're staying." Her blue eyes twinkled. "Oh, how my six-year-old heart broke when his family moved to Texas to start their own ranch." She grew quiet for a moment. "That was a long, long time ago. Big ranching is too hard for an old woman like me. Now, I just keep a few horses for people like you and your grandfather to come and ride."

"We're glad you do," said Jessie.

"And I started taking in rescue horses, trying to make them well," said Cookie.

"Does it cost a lot for people to adopt a rescue horse?" Violet asked.

Cookie looked surprised. "Why, Violet, we don't sell our horses. We give them away to good homes for free. I'm always trying to find people who want to adopt."

"We can help!" said Jessie. "We can put photos of the rescue horses on the Internet. That way, people all around the country can see them."

Cookie looked embarrassed. "I guess I should have done that a long time ago. Slim's the only one around here who's any good on the computer. He's always going online to buy the horses' medicines and such. I'm afraid that I'm not much good on the computer."

"We're good on the computer," said Jessie. "We'll teach you."

*   *   *

"Goldfish?" Benny bent over a big old

bathtub someone set in a pasture. Inside, swimming around the horse's drinking water, were several bright goldfish.

"Yup," said Bucky. He took off his hat with the feathers and wiped sweat off his forehead. "Horses are messy drinkers, always dropping in bits of grass and hay from their mouths. Also, mosquitoes lay their eggs in water. These goldfish love to eat all that stuff. They keep the drinking water clean and help cut down on mosquitoes."

Benny's eyes grew wide. "But . . . but don't the horses eat the fish?"

"Nope," said Bucky. "Watch." A colt and its mother walked over for a drink. As soon as they put their noses into the bathtub, all the fish swam to the other side and stayed up near the top. When the horses finished drinking, the goldfish swam back down in the tub. "Pretty good trick, huh?" said Bucky.

"My dog Watch does some tricks," said Benny. "But I didn't know you could train goldfish." He picked up the hose and added fresh water to the bathtub.

"Good job," said Bucky. He held his hand under the hose and wiped cold water over his face. "Where do you go next?"

Benny spread out the map and studied the Xes. He'd filled most of the water cans and buckets. But there were a few left before he reached the corral. "Here," he said, pointing.

"That's right," said Bucky. "You can finish the rest on your own. I've got to help unload the new shipment of feed. See you at lunch."

Benny felt very grown-up. He had to do an important job by himself. If he didn't water the horses, they would go thirsty. If they went thirsty, they'd get sick. He would not let them down. "See you tomorrow," he said to the goldfish, then ran to the next X on the map.

This X marked a small wooden shed with a fence around it. It was out in a pasture all by itself. As Benny unhooked the water bucket from the fence, a pony peeked out from the shed. It was all brown without a single speck of white or black. The mane between its ears stood straight up, like the bristles on Mrs. McGregor's scrub brush. "Hi, Brownie," said Benny. The brown pony tilted its head and stepped out of the stall. It watched Benny clean the bucket and fill it with water.

Benny accidentally splashed the pony. "Sorry, Brownie." The pony snorted.

Benny laughed. "I'll bet that water felt nice and cool."

A dark blue pickup truck rattled along the pasture road. It pulled a small silver trailer carrying two horses. The trailer was covered with little dinosaur stickers. Benny noticed that the front license plate had a picture of a cowboy on a bucking bronco. Benny tried to sound out the name of the state. It began with a W and had a "y" in it.

"Hey, kid," called the driver. He was a skinny man with bright red hair. Instead of a cowboy hat, he wore a white baseball cap turned backwards. The Adam's apple in his throat bobbed up and down like Slim's. "Which way to the main house?"

Benny opened his map and set it on the ground. He tried to figure out how to get to the main house from where they were.

"Come on," said the man, "I haven't got all day."

Benny pointed. "I . . . I think it's over that way." The man drove off without even saying thank you.

The brown pony snorted again. It looked hot. Benny pointed the hose at the sky. The spray fell like rain. The pony whinnied and stuck his nose in the spray. Then he walked right through. Then he walked through again.

"You'd like running through our sprinklers back home," said Benny. The water ran off the pony and onto the ground. It puddled around Benny's feet. Luckily, Benny wore the yellow rubber work boots Bucky gave him. He filled the pony's drinking bucket nice and full.

"See you tomorrow," he told the brown pony.

A breeze brought smells of something cooking. Benny's mouth watered. He hurried off to finish his work. Just a few more water buckets to clean and fill, and then he could dig into Cookie's delicious lunch.

Out in the pasture, Henry paced up and back along the broken fence. When was Kurt coming back with the tractor? It was boring just waiting around with nothing to do. He walked to the hole in the fence. Carefully, he stepped over the leaves, brown seed pods, and broken fence wire to the other side. A dirt path ran between the fence and the road. Henry saw hoofprints going out of the pasture onto the dirt. It looked like Kurt was right—Honey and Bunny had just walked away.

Alyssa rode up. "What did you find?" asked the wrangler. Henry showed her the hoofprints. She smiled with relief. "Thank goodness they weren't stolen."

"Why do people steal horses?" Henry asked.

"To sell, or else to keep for themselves without having to pay," Alyssa said. "I never thought it could happen here because we give our rescue horses away. Who would steal a horse that they could have for free?" She took off her red hat and used it to shoo flies from her horse's ears. "But when Honey and Bunny disappeared, and that woman brought flyers of her stolen horse . . . " Alyssa turned her horse around. "Thanks, Henry. Honey and Bunny won't have walked far. We'll find them." She rode away.

Henry walked farther, following the hoof-prints along the side of the road. Suddenly, the tracks stopped. Had the horses walked out onto the road? Henry looked, but there wasn't a single hoofprint there. He knelt down. Tire tracks began where the hoof-prints stopped.

Fear prickled the back of Henry's neck. His heart raced as he followed the tire tracks. Honey and Bunny *hadn't* wandered off! Someone had loaded them into a truck and stole them away. Henry ran back and untied Lightning from the tree. Then he rode as fast and as hard as he could to tell Kurt what he'd found.

...apped and cheered.

...y remembered the man with the ...red hair and big Adam's apple. "I saw ...said Benny. "He asked where the ranch ...was and I told him." He felt proud he ...elped.

..."Where did the man find the horses?" ...d Violet.

...he wrangler smiled. "In his pasture. ...saw Honey and Bunny grazing with his ...ses this morning."

..."Are they all right?" Jessie asked.

...Alyssa nodded. "Bucky is cleaning them up ...the stable, so after lunch, you can go and ...ay howdy."

Cookie came out of the kitchen carry-ing a plate heaped high with fresh-baked chocolate-chip, peanut butter, oatmeal raisin, and snickerdoodle cookies. The excited children quickly told her the good news about Honey and Bunny. Cookie looked puzzled.

"I didn't even know I had a new neighbor." She brightened. "I bet he bought the old Cedar Meadow Farm. I'll be sure to bring

CHAPTER 5

The Runaways Return

Clang, clang, clang. The metal cowbell rang out over the ranch. "Come and get it!" yelled Cookie. *Clang, clang, clang.*

The dining room quickly filled with hungry workers. Benny climbed in between Violet and Jessie.

"What happened to your boots?" asked Violet.

Benny looked down. His yellow boots were covered with brown stains. "I don't know," he said. He looked around the dining room.

"Where's Henry?" Benny asked.

"I'm sure he'll be here soon," said Jessie.

Cookie brought out bowls and plates of food. The children dug into big cups of chili served with fresh-baked corn bread. Benny heaped his plate with macaroni and cheese made with three creamy cheeses and baked until the top turned a crusty brown. Jessie cut a thick slice off a large meatloaf, then squirted ketchup on top. Violet filled a bowl with steaming vegetables picked fresh from Cookie's garden. She added a dollop of sweet butter, sprinkled on salt and pepper, and stirred it all around.

On every table, a giant platter overflowed with celery and carrot sticks, tomato and cucumber slices, and strips of zucchini and peppers. Baskets of fresh-baked biscuits were passed with apple butter, homemade jams, and pitchers of gravy.

Alyssa burst into the dining room and let out a shrill whistle. "I have great news," she said. "Honey and Bunny are home. A new neighbor just brought them back." The ranch

him a big thank-you box of my homemade cookies."

As Benny licked cinnamon sugar from the top of a snickerdoodle, he told the girls about the goldfish that lived in the horse's drinking water. Jessie and Violet described how hard it was to get horses to stand still to have their pictures taken.

Cookie set down a bowl of fresh fruit. "Did you have a chance to photograph the horses in the west pasture?"

"More horses?" exclaimed the girls.

"Not too many," said Cookie. "I never took you riding in the west pasture. You have to ride through a big hay field, and there's not much to see. There's an old barn out there we didn't use for years and years. It was Slim's idea to use it for all the rescue horses people send him. He brought in a couple of his own volunteers to help him out. We're lucky to find a vet that takes such good care of his patients." She plucked a grape from the bowl and popped it in her mouth. "So, do you think you gals have the energy to take more photos?" Cookie asked.

"Aren't we ever going to get to ride?" moaned Benny.

"Soon," Cookie said. "We need to finish a few more chores. I'll ring the bell when it's time to saddle up."

Jessie rumpled her little brother's hair. "Come help us," she said. "You can feed apples and carrots to the horses so they'll hold still."

"I'm good at that," said Benny. He followed his sisters into the big ranch kitchen. Violet took apples from a barrel and cut them into chunks. Benny found a crate of carrots and stuffed big bunches into a bag.

"You'd better change shoes," Violet told Benny. He ran to the stable and took off the yellow boots. He put them with the yellow boots the ranch hands used when they worked around water and mud. Benny's were the only pair with brown stains. "Hurry up," called Jessie. Benny pulled on his cowboy boots and ran out of the stable. Then the three children headed out across the ranch toward the west pasture.

They had walked five minutes when a horse and rider came toward them. "It's Henry," cried Benny, waving.

Henry pulled Lightning to a stop. "I found where Honey and Bunny got out!" In a rush, Henry told them about the broken fence and the hoofprints in the dirt, and the tire tracks. "I think someone saw Honey and Bunny on the road, then stole them."

Violet laughed. "No, no. A neighbor found them in his pasture and brought them home."

Henry frowned. "But . . . but I *saw* their hoofprints. I *saw* the tire tracks."

The four children tried to puzzle this out.

"Maybe there just happened to be tire tracks near the fence," said Violet. "People could have stopped to look at the broken fence after the horses got out. They could have driven over the horse's prints and erased them. That would explain why you couldn't see them."

Henry patted Lightning's neck. "That's what Kurt said. He said the hoofprints stopped because the horses wandered onto the road."

Jessie looked at her brother. "You don't think so, do you?"

Henry blew out a huff of air. "It just seems a great big coincidence to find a broken fence, hoofprints, *and* tire tracks all in the same place. And I don't like coincidences. But if Honey and Bunny are back, then I guess they weren't stolen." He noticed Jessie's camera and the big bag Benny was carrying. "Where are you going?"

"To photograph horses in the west pasture," said Violet.

"You'd better hurry and eat lunch," said Benny, "before the food's all gone."

Henry smiled at the thought of Cookie ever running out of food. "See you in a little while." Then he and Lightning took off across the field.

*   *   *

Henry walked Lightning into the stable. Bucky was washing a stout horse with a giant sponge. Another stout horse stood tied near-by. Bucky's hat with the feathers hung on a nail in the wall, and his cowboy boots stood under it. He wore yellow rubber boots while he slopped soapy water on the horse.

"Did you and Kurt mend the fence?" Bucky asked.

"Yes." Henry unbuckled Lightning's saddle and set it on the saddle stand. Then he took off his riding helmet and hung it on the wall.

Bucky frowned at Henry's face and arms. "Where'd you get all scratched up like that?"

"Tying rope around that broken tree branch."

"Better wash those cuts so they don't get infected," said Bucky. "By the way," he said, patting the soapy horse, "this here's Honey, and that there's Bunny."

Henry ran his hand over Honey's smooth hide. "How did she get out of the pasture without that tree branch scratching her up?"

"She must've walked around it," said Bucky.

"No way," said Henry. He searched but he couldn't find a single scratch or scrape on either horse. "I could barely squeeze between the branch and the fence post, and I'm a lot skinnier than these two."

"An *elephant's* skinnier than these two," said Bucky, laughing.

"Who brought them back?" Henry asked.

"Some neighbor from up the road." Bucky squinted one eye. "I don't recall seeing him before. 'Course, I've been gone from here a lot of years. Moved away when I was around eight years old. Most of the people I used to know are long gone."

"Henry Alden!" Cookie strode into the stable. "If you don't get some food in your belly right this minute, your grandfather will have my hide. Bucky, are you keeping this boy from his lunch?"

Bucky's face turned bright red. Even the tips of his ears looked on fire against his white hair. He looked down at the ground where his boots were getting muddy from the running hose. "Sorry," he said. "Didn't mean to."

"Come on, Henry," Cookie said, "I'll heat some food for you. We have a long afternoon's work ahead of us." As they walked out, Cookie glanced back at Bucky and, Henry thought, Cookie's face seemed to turn a bit redder, too.

CHAPTER 6

Disappearing Dragon

"Easy, girl. That's a good horse. Nice horse." Violet spoke softly to each horse as Benny fed them carrots and apples. Jessie took the pictures. There were few horses in the west pasture, and the three children quickly took one photo after another.

They were nearly done when a dark blue pickup truck slowed near the fence. It pulled a small silver trailer. Two horses inside swished their tails side-to-side. The trailer covered the front halves of the horses. But the children saw the backsides of a big black horse and a small brown pony.

"Look," Benny cried, "that's the neighbor who brought back Honey and Bunny."

"Hey!" A cowboy in a striped shirt galloped up and jerked his horse to a stop. "What are you kids doing here?"

Jessie smiled. "We're taking pictures of all the horses for—"

"Not *these* horses," growled the man.

"Cookie asked us to," said Violet.

"No one's allowed out here."

Benny folded his arms across his chest. "Why not?"

"Because . . . because . . . " The man wiggled his jaw from side to side for a moment. "Ah, because we got new rescue horses comin' in. They're, ah, sick. They could, um, bite you. No one's allowed out here but us . . . us volunteers." His horse pawed the ground, eyeing a piece of apple Benny had dropped. The man glowered at Jessie. "What are those pictures for?"

Jessie brightened. "Well, you see, we're going to put them on the Inter—"

Suddenly, the man's horse jerked its head down, yanking the man forward. A large yellow envelope fell out of the man's shirt pocket onto the ground. Money spilled out. He jumped off his horse and grabbed the envelope, shoving the bills back inside. Then he tucked the envelope back in his shirt and climbed on his horse. The man reached for Jessie's camera. "I'll take your pictures, girlie," he said, "and bring them to you later."

In the distance, a cowbell rang. "No, thank you," said Jessie, clutching her brand new birthday camera. She would not leave it with someone she didn't know. The cowbell rang again.

"We have to go," said Violet. "It's time for our ride."

And with that, the three children ran off across the west pasture, through the fence and field of tall hay, and didn't slow until they were a good distance away.

"He *really* didn't want us taking pictures," said Jessie.

"That's 'cause the horses might bite us," said Benny. He took the last carrot out of the bag, munching happily as they walked.

"If you ask me," Violet said, "the only thing those horses wanted to bite were carrots and apples."

The cowbell rang again and the three children ran as fast as they could across the pasture toward the corral. At last they would get the chance to ride.

Jessie stopped in the ranch house to put her camera in Cookie's office. She quickly plugged it into Cookie's computer. She typed in "Jessie's File," and copied her horse photos from the camera to the computer. Tonight, after dinner, she would teach Cookie how to post the rescue horse photos on the Dare to Dream Website.

Clang, clang, clang, went the dinner bell.

Jessie unplugged her camera and set it carefully on the shelf above the computer. Then she ran out to the corral to saddle Dragon.

But Dragon wasn't in the corral. Jessie ran out to the pasture. In the distance, Bucky stood next to the fence surrounded by several horses. "Have you seen Dragon?" called Jessie.

"Not since this morning," he called back. He took off his feathered hat. "Eeeeeee-haaaa!" he yelled, waving his hat at the horses, shooing them back into the pasture. A couple of orange feathers floated out. "Maybe he's still in the stable."

Jessie ran to the stable, but Dragon's stall was empty. Jessie's stomach did a flip-flop. Something was wrong. She found Alyssa in the corral, saddling the horses for their ride. "I can't find Dragon," said Jessie.

"Oh, he's here somewhere," said the wrangler. "Sometimes Dragon wanders off. He likes to explore. We should have named him Christopher Columbus." She saw the worry on Jessie's face. "He'll turn up," said Alyssa. "He always does. Meanwhile, you can ride Jumpin' Jack here. He's a real sweetie."

*   *   *

Alyssa led the children on the long trail that wound along the ranch fence. "Benny," said the wrangler. "Try not to hold onto the saddle horn. Cowboys hold the reins with their hands and grip the horse with their knees." Slowly, Benny let go of the horn. He squeezed the saddle with his knees. It felt scary not to hold on. But he wanted to learn to ride like a real cowboy.

Henry rode next to Jessie. "Don't be sad," he said.

She patted Jumpin' Jack's neck. "I'm worried about Dragon. What if he's been stolen?"

"He's not stolen," said Henry, trying to make her feel better.

"Then where *is* he?" Jessie asked.

But Henry had no answer.

They rode past the fence where Bucky had been shooing the horses. Lots-o'-Dots sniffed the air. Suddenly, he jerked his head to the left and trotted toward the fence.

"Whoa!" cried Benny. The small boy leaned back, pulling on the reins with all his might, but Lots-o'-Dots kept going. The little horse went straight to the fence and bent his head to the ground. Benny tugged and tugged, but Lots-o'-Dots wouldn't budge.

Jessie climbed down to see what Benny's horse had found. "Look," she said, picking up a handful of grain. "Someone dumped oats in the grass."

Alyssa rode over. "What's the problem?"

"Lots-o'-Dots found some oats to eat," said Benny.

"Who would put oats so close to the fence?" asked Henry.

"Tourists." Alyssa took off her red hat to shoo flies off her horse. "All summer, city folks stop to give treats to our horses—sugar cubes, carrots, apples. You'd think they never saw a horse before. Though this is the first time I've seen them bring oats." She looked at the children. "Would anybody like to do a little cantering?"

"Yes!" they all cheered. For they loved to ride fast, and a canter was almost as fast as a full-out run.

Alyssa grabbed Lots-o'-Dot's reins and led

him back to the trail. "Let's ride!" she said.
And, tapping their horses with their heels,
the eager group took off, cantering across
the sprawling ranch.

As they rode, Jessie looked for Dragon.
She didn't see him anywhere. They rode and
rode, across pastures and through fields of tall
hay, over hills, and past stands of towering
pines until they reached a far pasture. Three
enormous trees grew there.

Alyssa held her hand up high. It was the
signal to stop. The children pulled back on
their reins and walked their horses into the
trees' cool shade.

"This is where I helped fix the broken
fence," Henry said, proudly, pointing toward
the road. "I dug in those two new posts and
helped Kurt string the wire."

"Let's give our horses a rest." Alyssa said.
"You can stretch your legs."

Violet took her sketchpad and pencil from
her saddlebag. She was eager to begin plan-
ning her mural. These trees and horses would
look beautiful painted on the side of the barn.

Near the fence, she picked up a long brown pod. Last year, for a school science project, she collected leaves from her neighborhood. She glued them onto construction paper and stitched the pages into a book called *The Trees of Greenfield*. "This is from a honey locust," she said, shaking the pod. The seeds inside rattled.

"That fell off of the branch that broke the fence," said Henry.

Violet looked at the three big trees. There were no other trees nearby. "These are maples," she said. "There's no honey locust here."

"Kurt said a wind must have blown the branch down," Henry replied.

"That must have been one strong wind," Violet said.

Benny lay in the shade of a tree, staring straight up. "Why does this tree have holes in it?" he asked.

"Remember our trip to Canada?" asked Jessie. "At the sugar camp, we saw people drill holes like these into maple trees, then hook buckets under each hole."

"The syrup ran out of the trees into the buckets!" said Benny.

Alyssa nodded. "Some of that maple syrup you ate on your flapjacks came right from these three maple trees."

"And," added Henry, "cowboys leave notes in these holes."

Alyssa laughed. "I never heard *that* one before."

Henry walked around the tree but the note he'd found about the gray Arabian and brown spotted pony was gone.

Something floated down from the tree. "Helicopters!" Benny picked up a small seed pod shaped like an *8*. He threw the pod high into the air. As it floated down, it spun around and around, like the blades of a helicopter. Soon, the others scurried around, gathering "helicopters" to launch into flight. Benny stuffed a bunch into his pocket to play with later.

*   *   *

After a rest, they rode back toward the corral. When they reached the fence where the oats had been, Henry rode over. He studied the wire nailed to the fencepost. "Look," he said. "Fence wire should be twisted nice and tight so it can't open. But this wire has loops on the end that are hooked around bent nails." He climbed off Lightning and lifted the fence wire off of the nails. The fence opened like a gate. Henry knelt down, studying the ground.

"What are you looking for?" asked Jessie.

"Hoofprints," Henry said. And sure enough they saw horse tracks leading out of the pasture onto the dirt. Once again, the horseshoe prints ended where tire tracks began. Shivers ran up Jessie's neck. Now she knew why she couldn't find Dragon in the corral or the pasture. Now she understood why Dragon wasn't in his stall. Alyssa had been wrong. Dragon wasn't out exploring.

Tears mixed with anger as Jessie stared at the hoofprint that had one square toe. "Dragon," Jessie whispered. "Someone stole Dragon!"

CHAPTER 7

The Secret File

The children sat on the corral fence. Cookie and Bucky stood next to them, looking grim. Jessie sniffed, her eyes puffy from crying.

"Let me get this straight," the policeman said. "This morning you told me that two of your horses were stolen. But then they came back?"

"Yes. A neighbor brought them," said Cookie. "It turns out they weren't stolen. They'd wandered off through a hole in the fence where a tree branch had fallen."

Henry didn't say anything. But he wondered why Honey and Bunny weren't all scratched up from the tree branch, the way he was. And how had that heavy locust branch been blown so far? "Now," the policeman said, "another horse is missing."

This time, Henry did speak up. "Dragon was stolen for sure," he said. "Those were his shoe prints outside the fence."

"And the fence was rigged so it could be secretly opened and closed," said Jessie.

"*And* someone dumped oats!" added Benny, "to make horses come to the fence. Horses love oats!"

"We think the thief unhooked the wire, stole Dragon, and then put the wire back," said Violet.

The policeman jotted a few notes. "Who saw Dragon last?"

"I put Dragon in his stall after breakfast," said Bucky. "Jessie here wanted to ride him.

But Kurt said his leg was still bad. I put Dragon in his stall so the vet could take a look. That was the last time I saw him."

"Has anyone talked to the vet?"

No one had. "Slim drove by when I was fixing the fence," said Henry. "He was on his way to buy medicine for the horses."

The policeman lifted one eyebrow at Cookie. "There's lots of people working here," he said. "Ranch hands, volunteers, these kids. Seems to me someone would notice horse thievery going on."

"It was lunchtime," said Cookie. "Everyone was in the dining room."

The policeman pushed back his hat. "How would a thief know you'd all be eating?"

"I clang that lunch bell so loud you can hear it halfway to China," said Cookie. "Whoever stole Dragon knew they had a lot of time to do it."

"So everyone was in the dining room," the policeman said.

"I wasn't," said Bucky. "I was in the stable cleaning up Honey and Bunny."

"And Alyssa came in late," said Jessie.

"Kurt and I weren't there, either," said Henry. "We were fixing a broken fence."

"All right," the policeman flipped to a fresh page. "What does this horse look like?"

"He's black with a big white patch on his back that looks like a dragon," said Jessie. "Wait! I have a photo!" She jumped down from the fence. "I'll print it out for you."

She ran to the office to get her camera. It wasn't on the shelf over the computer. But she was *sure* she left it there. Jessie looked under papers on the desk, then under the desk. She searched the cluttered shelves filled with horse trophies and horse magazines and books. Gone! Her camera was gone.

Her mind raced. *The computer!* She'd copied the photos on Cookie's computer. Jessie raced over and turned it on. "Please be here," she said, "please, please, *please.*"

The dark screen turned blue and Jessie crossed her fingers as the files appeared. Finally, "Jessie's File," came up. She clicked on it and the screen filled with small photos of each horse. There was Lots-o'-Dots and Lightning; Daisy and Jumpin' Jack. She looked and looked, but Dragon was not there. Then she remembered—Bucky had taken Dragon to the stable *before* Jessie began taking pictures.

Violet and Benny came in. "Did you find Dragon's picture?"

"I never took it," said Jessie. "And my camera is missing."

Violet gasped. "Are you sure?"

Jessie nodded. "Luckily, I made a copy of our photos on Cookie's computer." She began typing. "I'll hide the photos where a thief won't find them." She made a file called *Maple Syrup Recipes* and moved all the horse photos inside. "No one will look for horses inside a Maple Syrup Recipe file." She turned off the computer. "Let's go break the bad news."

"I'll meet you at the corral," said Violet, heading for the bunkhouse. "I need to get something." She ran off before they could ask what it was.

At the corral, Jessie told everyone about the stolen camera.

"Tarnation!" thundered Cookie. "You're saying a thief was in my house?" She stood nose-to-nose with the policeman. "You need to find that camera-stealing, horse-stealing, good-for-nothing, no-account—" Her face grew red.

"Easy there," said Bucky, patting her shoulder. But that just made Cookie's face turn redder.

"Who saw you taking pictures of the horses?" the policeman asked.

"Everyone who passed the corral," said Jessie. "Wranglers, volunteers. And there was a man in the west pasture. A volunteer in a striped shirt. He said it was too dangerous for us to be out there."

"That's one of Slim's helpers," said Bucky. "The vet trains them to care for the sickest of the rescue horses. We don't even see those horses until Slim says they're well enough to come here to the corral. Slim's helpers live at the old bunkhouse in the west pasture. They never come up here to the house, so they couldn't steal your camera."

Violet ran up. "Here," she said, holding up a sketch of a horse.

"Dragon!" cried Jessie. "Oh, Violet, it looks just like him."

"I was—" Violet gasped for breath, "I was drawing it—for your birthday— surprise."

"It *is* a wonderful surprise," said Jessie, hugging her sister. She showed the drawing to the policeman. "This is our missing horse. This is Dragon. Please help us find him."

The policeman took the drawing and promised to see what he could do. The small group watched the police car pull away. "I know you're upset," said Cookie. "I am, too. But right now, you need to go tend to your horses."

"But . . . but what about Dragon?" asked Jessie.

"When you live on a ranch," said Cookie, "even if the sky is falling, the animals need to be watered and fed and groomed. That doesn't stop for anything. Not ever. You all rode your horses hard. They're tired. Bucky will teach you how to groom them. When you finish, I'll drive you around to the neighbors. Maybe someone has seen Dragon."

*   *   *

In the corral, the children took off their cowboy boots. They put on yellow rubber boots to keep their feet dry. Then they washed and groomed their horses. Jessie brushed Jumpin' Jack. How she wished he were Dragon! Next to her, Henry combed a tangle of small leaves from Lightning's tail. "It will be all right," he told his sister. "We'll find Dragon."

Nearby, Violet braided Daisy's mane with ribbons. "You look beautiful," she said, running her hand down Daisy's shiny coat.

"Lots-o'-Dots looks great, too," said Benny. The little horse's coat gleamed from brushing.

Bucky walked around them, inspecting each child's work. "You're doing a great job," he said. "Now, here's how to clean your horse's hooves." Gently, Bucky ran one hand down Lightning's leg and lifted the foot. "You know how it hurts to have a sliver in your foot?" he asked. The children nodded. "Well, horses get things stuck in their hooves. You need to pick them out." He showed them how. "When you finish, turn your horses out to pasture. They could use a little rest before your evening ride. I've got some work that needs doing." He climbed on his horse, and rode off.

Carefully, the children picked dirt and stones and twigs from their horses' hooves. "Wow!" said Benny, holding up something small and shiny. "This was stuck in Lots-o'-Dots's hoof."

Violet took it and held it up to the light. "It's a glass bead," she said. "Like the ones I string into necklaces."

Benny cleaned a second hoof. "Here's another one. And another!" By the time Benny finished, he found six beads. "Where did you get these?" he asked his horse. But

Lots-o'-Dots wasn't telling.

When the children finished, they ran to the house to get Cookie. "I'm in here," she called from the office.

"We're ready to go look for Dragon," they said.

"I need a little more time." Cookie worked at the computer. A tall stack of blank yellow paper sat on her desk. "I phoned the policeman who was here and had him fax this to me." She held up a copy of Violet's sketch of Dragon. "I'm making up flyers we can pass out to people. But it will take me about an hour."

"An *hour!*" cried Benny, who hated to wait. For *anything*.

Cookie gave him a hug. "I hate waiting, too," she said. "When I was your age, my best friend Trevor and I went to town every Sunday for ice cream. The days from Sunday to Sunday seemed to take forever."

She started typing. STOLEN HORSE, she wrote, then she paused. "This hour will go faster if you keep busy," she told the children. "Violet, maybe you can work on your drawing for the barn mural. And Benny, there's an old bike behind the barn. You can ride around the ranch to see of any of the horses need more water. Jessie and Henry, you can muck out a few of the stable stalls."

"Muck?" said Jessie.

"It means cleaning the stalls, clearing old bedding from the floors, scrubbing the walls, putting in fresh sand and hay. I'll ring the cowbell when the flyers are ready."

The children immediately set about their tasks. Violet took out her sketch of the horses grazing under the three big maple trees. She would add helicopter seeds to her drawing, as a surprise for Benny. And she would put in a honey locust with long brown pods.

Violet frowned. She couldn't remember seeing a locust tree at all. That was odd— there had to be one. How else could a locust branch fall on the fence? Henry said a strong wind blew it down. But a strong wind would have broken branches off many different trees, and she hadn't seen any. She would look again more closely the next time they rode out that way.

In the stable, Jessie and Henry got to work cleaning. Jessie loaded a broom and pitchfork into a wheelbarrow and walked to Dragon's empty stall. "Where are you?" she whispered, her heart heavy. She forked the old straw bedding into the wheelbarrow, then swept the floor clean. Then she turned on the hose and scrubbed the walls. In a dark corner, someone had carved a small heart into the wood with the initials *TA + LM*. She showed it to Henry.

"I saw a heart just like that cut into a maple tree," he said. "Maybe Cookie will know who TA and LM are."

The two children carried in a bale of fresh straw and spread it on the floor. "We'll find you," Jessie whispered as they left Dragon's stall. "I promise."

*   *   *

Benny pedaled the rickety bike around the ranch. He rode to every *X* on the map, adding water to buckets that needed it, stopping to say hello to the goldfish. His last stop was the brown pony's shed.

"Hey, Brownie," called Benny. But, this time, the little pony didn't peek out. Benny turned on the hose and pointed the water at the sky. "It's raining, it's pouring," he sang. Still, no brown pony. Benny climbed through the fence. Near the shed, he smelled something familiar, like when Grandfather polished his shoes.

"Brownie?" he said, walking inside. But the pony wasn't inside. An empty bottle of brown shoe polish lay in the straw on the ground. Were you supposed to polish a horse's shoes? He didn't think so. And where was the little pony? Did someone steal him, too?

Benny jumped on the bike, pedaling hard toward the ranch. As he reached the top of a hill, he saw Slim the vet walking a big white horse. "Have you seen Brownie?" asked Benny.

The vet furrowed his brow. "Brownie?" he asked.

"The little brown pony in the shed," said

Benny. "I call him Brownie."

"Oh, oh, yes, Brownie. He's, um, he's been adopted. The family picked him up just a while ago," said Slim.

Benny remembered the trailer carrying a brown pony and big black horse. He thought it belonged to the neighbor who brought Honey and Bunny home. But it must have been Brownie's new family. "I'm glad he wasn't stolen like Dragon," Benny said.

The smile vanished from Slim's face. "What?"

"Someone stole Dragon," Benny said.

The vet cleared his throat. "Why, that's terrible." His Adam's apple jumped up and down. "Who would do such a terrible thing?"

"We told the police and we're going to pass out flyers," Benny told him.

"Really?" Slim took out a handkerchief and wiped sweat off his face. "So everyone will be looking for Dragon. Why, that's wonderful." A loud horn blasted as an eighteen-wheel truck barreled along the road near the ranch.

At first, Benny thought it was a moving van. Then he saw big holes all along the sides. "What kind of truck is that?" he asked.

"Truck?" said Slim, "Hmmm. Looks like a cattle truck. Moves cows from one place to another. Those holes let air in so they can breathe. Yup. Cattle truck. Well, I'd better get Lucy here back to the old corral." He started walking away.

"Why don't you ride your horse?" Benny asked.

The vet's eyebrows shot up. "Ride? Why, yes. Love to ride. I was born in the saddle. Heh-heh." He put one foot in the stirrup and tried to climb on the horse but it kept walking around and around in circles. Slim hopped, one foot up in the stirrup and the other foot on the ground. "Easy, girl. Oh-oh. Easy, now." Around and around he hopped. Finally, Slim hauled himself up into the saddle.

"See you later," he said. And gripping the saddle horn tightly with both hands—the way Alyssa had told Benny *not* to—Slim bumped along toward the west pasture.

The cowbell rang. Benny jumped on his bike and peddled to the stable. He and Jessie and Henry quickly changed out of their work boots into their cowboy boots. Jessie set their yellow boots on the rack. "Our boots have stains, just like Benny's," she said. "Except his are brown and ours are black."

Where did the stains come from? They looked down the long narrow stable. Stalls lined both sides. The ground was wet in front of the stalls Jessie and Henry had washed down. A dark stain ran out of Dragon's stall. Henry bent down and touched it. "It smells like shoe polish."

"I saw shoe polish in Brownie's shed," said Benny.

"Maybe cowboys use it to shine the saddles," Jessie said. "Or their boots."

The bell rang again. The children hurried to Cookie's car. It was time to search for Dragon.

Cookie and the children drove from ranch to ranch, farm to farm, house to house, handing out flyers. In town, they put flyers in all the store windows. Cookie treated them to a quick dinner at Big Herm's Hot Dog Palace, and then they went back to work.

They tacked flyers on the bulletin boards at the library, the community center, and the sheriff's office. They slipped them under the windshield wipers of cars parked at the grocery store and shopping center.

It was late when they finally pulled into the Dare to Dream Ranch.

"Do you think our flyers will help find Dragon?" Jessie asked.

"I hope so," said Henry.

CHAPTER 8

A Flashlight Night

The children lay awake in their bunks. One hour passed. And another. But sleep would not come. Henry's back was sore from digging the fence posts. His face and arms stung from the locust branch scratches.

Violet thought about the woman whose horse, Buttercup, was stolen. She thought about the flyers and hoped her drawing of Dragon was good enough to help find him.

Jessie's pillow was wet with tears. Who

would steal Dragon? Was he all right?

Benny thought about the goldfish in the horse's drinking water. He thought about the little brown pony who liked being sprinkled with the hose. He thought about the skinny red-haired man who brought Honey and Bunny home.

"What license plate has a picture of a cowboy riding a bucking bronco?" he asked. Benny forgot he was supposed to be sleeping.

Henry peered down from his bunk. "Where did you see that?" he whispered.

"On the blue pickup truck that brought Honey and Bunny back." Benny closed his eyes and pictured the license plate. "The state's name had a *W* and a *Y* in it."

"Wyoming," whispered Violet.

"Is Wyoming near Connecticut?" asked Benny.

Jessie groaned. As soon as Benny could read a little better, she would teach him geography. "Wyoming is halfway across the

United States from here," she said. "When we get home, I'll show you on the map."

"I guess we're awake," said Henry, switching on his flashlight. Three more flashlights switched on. Henry flashed his light at Jessie. "Didn't you tell me a *neighbor* brought Honey and Bunny back?"

"Yes." Jessie sniffed. "Alyssa said the man found them in his pasture."

Henry clicked his flashlight on and off. "Why would a neighbor here in Connecticut have *Wyoming* license plates?"

The children chased each other's lights around the ceiling. "Cookie said she didn't know this neighbor," said Violet. "That he must have just moved here."

"That could explain the Wyoming plates," agreed Henry. "Come to think of it, Bucky told me he never saw the neighbor before."

Jessie swooped big circles around the wall with her light. "What do we really know about Bucky? When I went looking for Dragon, I saw Bucky standing near the fence with a bunch of horses. What if *he* spilled the oats so the horses would come to the fence? What if *he* rigged that fence to open?" A shiver went through her. "Dragon could have gone to eat the oats, and a friend of Bucky's could have come and stolen him."

"Bucky told me he grew up around here," said Henry. "He moved away when he was eight, and he just came back."

Benny held his flashlight under his chin. It made him look scary. "Maybe Bucky came back to steal Cookie's horses," he said.

Violet traced her light along the ceiling. Suddenly, she sat up, gasping. "I just thought of something."

"What, what?" they all demanded.

"Okay, pretend we wake up tomorrow morning and find a strange dog right here in the bunkhouse. How do we know who it belongs to?"

"Dog tags?" asked Benny.

"No tags," said Violet. "Just dog."

"Then, we wouldn't know whose dog it was," said Jessie. "We don't live around here."

"Exactly!"

"So?" asked Benny.

"Sooooo," said Violet, "the man who brought Honey and Bunny back said he found them in his pasture. But he's never been to the Dare to Dream Ranch. How did he know they belonged here?"

"Horse tags?" said Benny, giggling. He always giggled when it was far past his bedtime.

"I'm serious," Violet said.

"He couldn't have known," said Jessie. "What if he's not a neighbor at all? What if he's a thief?"

"He's not," Henry yawned. "Because thieves steal things." He yawned again, which made everyone else yawn. "Thieves don't bring things back."

"Like the thief who stole my new camera," said Jessie.

"I'll bet it was that man out at the old barn," said Benny. "He didn't like you taking pictures of the rescue horses."

"It can't be him," said Violet. "Cookie

said that Slim's volunteers stay out at the old barn. They never come to the main house. The camera thief has to be someone who wouldn't look suspicious walking into Cookie's office."

"Like Cookie?" asked Benny. The others groaned. "Like us?"

Violet sighed. "It would have to be someone who comes in and out a lot, like Slim or Alyssa, Kurt or Bucky."

Henry yawned. "I saw Slim driving off to buy medicine for the horses," he said. "So it couldn't be him. But I don't know where Kurt went after we fixed the fence. And I don't know where Alyssa was before she took us on the trail ride. And Bucky could have been anywhere."

The children felt sad. They didn't want to accuse someone they knew of stealing the camera. But none of them could think who else it might be.

The weary children switched off their flash-lights and pulled their blankets tight. One by one they fell fast asleep. Benny struggled to stay awake. But his eyelids finally grew heavy, too.

*   *   *

Smoke! The smell of it woke the children at dawn. They leapt from their bunks and ran to the window. "There!" cried Violet, pointing to an orange glow in the distance. They raced to the ranch house to tell Cookie. She was already busy in the kitchen baking biscuits for breakfast.

"It's all right," she told them. "Kurt and the men are at the fire pit. Every few days, they burn brush at sunup, when the air is still. That keeps the fire from spreading. If you like, you can ride out and take a look-see before breakfast."

The children quickly dressed and saddled up, then rode out across the ranch until they reached a big open field. A powerful fire roared in the middle. Ranch hands tossed old branches and brush into the flames. They wore kerchiefs over their mouths and noses. Kurt drove a tractor in a wide circle around and around the fire. A big rake hooked to the back of his tractor raked the dirt to keep the fire from spreading. The children's horses snorted and backed up nervously. "This must be where Kurt brought the locust branch that crushed the fence," said Henry.

Violet thought of her sketch. "Henry," she said, "there are only three big trees near that fence. And they are all maple trees. There isn't a locust anywhere near there. Someone brought the locust branch there. Someone dropped it on the fence."

They watched Kurt driving the tractor. The ranch manager saw the children and drove over. He pulled his kerchief down. His face was sooty from the smoke. The ends of his blond moustache drooped from the heat.

"Get those horses away from here," he said, scowling. "Did Alyssa send you out here?"

"Alyssa?" asked Jessie.

Kurt snorted in disgust. "She doesn't even know that horses can panic around smoke. She's the worst wrangler I've ever seen. If Cookie had hired my friend for the job, this ranch would be run right! Now, get those horses away from here." He pulled up his kerchief and drove the tractor back to the fire.

The children rode slowly back to the ranch house. "Do you think Kurt turned Honey and Bunny loose?" asked Jessie. "To make it look like Alyssa couldn't take care of the horses?"

"He did blame her for letting them escape," said Violet.

Henry looked at the scratches on his hands. "Honey and Bunny didn't have any scratches. Which means they escaped *before* the branch fell on the fence. Kurt could have cut the fence wire, turned the horses loose, then dropped the branch on the fence."

"And maybe he stole Dragon to make Alyssa look even worse," said Jessie.

"Shouldn't we tell Cookie?" asked Violet.

"We have no proof," Henry said. "We need to think of a way to find some."

CHAPTER 9

A Computer Connection

"Did anyone call about Dragon?" asked the children as they walked in to breakfast.

"Not yet," said Cookie. "But it's still early. Not everyone has seen our flyers." The children ate quietly, then went to do their chores. "Please, ring the cowbell if anyone calls," said Jessie.

"I will," promised Cookie. All morning, the children listened for the bell, but it didn't ring until it called the ranch hands to lunch.

At lunchtime, Cookie set a big platter of

chicken on the table. "I talked to a friend who works at the newspaper. He said I should bring him one of our flyers and he'll put it in tomorrow's paper." She pressed her lips together. "He said a couple of other people have called him the past few days about missing horses. It looks like horse thieves might be working in this area."

The children stared at the food in their plates. Not even Benny was hungry.

Cookie wiped her hands on her apron. "Today is Alyssa's day off, but you four can go on a ride by yourselves after lunch. It will help take your minds off Dragon. I'll bring the flyer over to the newspaper." She took off her apron. "Try to eat a little something," she said, leaving. "I'll see you later."

Benny nibbled a chicken leg. Henry made a sandwich from the peanut butter and jelly Cookie kept on the table. Violet sipped vegetable soup. Jessie pushed a cucumber around her plate. "It's so hard to sit here doing nothing," Jessie said. Suddenly, she jumped up. "I know what we can do!" And with that, she ran to Cookie's office and turned on the computer. The others gathered around as she typed in the words "Stolen Horses." The screen filled with websites listing missing horses. Jessie typed Dragon's description on one website after another.

Every time Jessie went to a new website, the children looked at the photos of missing horses. Some of the horses had been found. Some were still missing. Jessie clicked to a new website. Violet gasped. "Oh!" she said, pointing to a photo.

"It's Lots-o'-Dots!" cried Benny. Sure enough, there on the screen was Benny's little spotted horse. The writing under the photo said:

POLKY-DOTS
MISSING FOR ONE MONTH
from Edie's Bead Shop, Big Piney, Wyoming

Our friendly horse is so much more than a pet. Everyone who visited our little bead shop loved our funny little Polky-Dots. He often walked right through our shop to say "Howdy" to our customers. Polky-Dots loves his treats and will poke his nose right into your pocket looking for a sugar cube or apple or carrot. If you have seen our wonderful horse, please call Edie's Bead Shop.

"That's why he had beads stuck in his hooves," said Benny.

Henry picked up the phone and called the number for Edie's Bead Shop. A woman answered.

"I'm calling from the Dare to Dream Rescue Ranch," Henry told her. "Polky-Dots is safe and happy." The children heard the woman laughing and crying. "Polky-Dots must have wandered away from your place," Henry explained. "Then someone rescued him and sent him here." Henry listened for a few minutes. His smile disappeared.

"What's wrong?" asked Jessie, as he hung up the phone.

Henry looked troubled. "The woman said Lots-o'-Dots didn't walk away. She said someone broke into her barn and stole him last month."

Jessie pointed to the address on the screen. "Edie's Bead Shop is in Wyoming," she said.

"And Benny said the truck that brought Honey and Bunny back had Wyoming license plates."

"Was that truck pulling a small silver trailer with dinosaur stickers on it?" Henry asked.

Benny's mouth dropped open. "How did you know?"

Henry explained, "Because the thieves also stole the bead store owner's trailer. She said her little boy liked to decorate the trailer with dinosaur stickers."

Benny gulped. He'd been face to face with a horse thief and didn't even know it! He thought about the red-haired man with the backward baseball cap. "But the man wasn't stealing Honey and Bunny," said Benny. "He was bringing them back."

Henry paced the small office. Walking back and forth helped him think better. "Maybe," he said, "he wanted to throw us off the trail. Maybe he really wanted to steal Dragon. If we thought Honey and Bunny just walked away, we would think Dragon walked away, too."

Jessie looked at the computer picture of

Lots-o'-Dots. "Why would someone bring a stolen horse here to the ranch?"

Henry paced faster and faster. "What if the thief didn't bring Lots-o'-Dots here to stay? What if he's hiding him here until he can sell him?"

"Sell!" cried Violet. "Oh, Jessie, remember when we were taking pictures of horses in the west pasture and the man in the striped shirt tried to stop us? And an envelope full of money fell out of his pocket."

Henry stopped pacing. "What if the thief brought Lots-o'-Dots and other horses here to hide them until he can sell them? What better place to hide a horse than on a horse ranch?"

"Cookie said the west pasture hadn't been used in years," Jessie said. "Until Slim decided to use it for his rescue horses."

"Maybe the rescue horses need to be rescued," said Benny.

"Let's ride out there and take a look," said Henry. "Let's see what horses are out in the old barn."

Violet looked unsure. "Shouldn't we wait for Cookie?"

"She might not be back for hours," said Jessie. "What if stolen horses are in the old barn? What if Dragon is out there? The thieves could take him away by the time Cookie comes home. We have to go right now!"

They went to saddle their horses but Lots-o'-Dots was not in the corral. "Maybe he's in the pasture," Henry said. "We don't have time to look for him now." Henry quickly saddled another little horse for Benny.

The four children rode out across the ranch. They saw many horses grazing in the pastures. But Lots-o'-Dots wasn't among them.

Far off, in the west pasture, a long silver truck stood near the old barn. "I saw that truck before," Benny said. "It has holes in the side so the cows can breathe."

"It's a horse trailer, too" said Henry.

"It could be bringing in new rescue horses," said Violet.

"Or stolen ones," said Henry.

The children rode their horses through a field of tall hay toward the trailer. The truck's back gate was down. But, instead of taking horses off, the man in the striped shirt was loading a white horse onto the truck.

"I saw Slim riding that horse," said Benny. "Slim says he's a good rider. But he holds on to the saddle horn with both hands."

The man in the striped shirt gripped the horse's bridle. He pulled the horse up the ramp into the truck.

"That's the man who yelled at us for taking pictures," said Violet.

Henry held up his hand. Everyone stopped. The man went back into the barn and soon led out a beautiful gray horse with a white patch on its nose. Its tail was white and black.

"That's Buttercup," whispered Jessie, "the stolen horse on the purple flyer! She's been here the whole time!"

"We need to get closer," Henry said, "but I don't want that man to see us." Henry climbed off his horse and let go of the reins.

He motioned the others to do the same. The horses walked off.

"They'll run away," said Benny.

"They'll look for a place to graze," said Henry. "We'll find them later."

The children crouched low, moving silently through the tall hay. Soon, they were close to the barn.

"Come *on*, you stubborn horse!" a man growled. The children fell to their stomachs so that they were hidden by the hay. They peered out as a man tugged a big black horse out of the barn.

Jessie's hands flew to her mouth. "Dragon!"

"Where?" Benny whispered.

"Right there." The horse was all black. There was no big white dragon on its back. "I'm telling you, it's Dragon," said Jessie.

"The shoe polish," said Henry. "They used that black shoe polish to cover his white dragon. That way, even if someone saw him, they wouldn't recognize him."

"I would," said Jessie. "I'd know him anywhere."

Dragon wouldn't get into the truck. He reared up, whinnying. The man yanked the reins. "Come on!" he shouted. "Git in there!" He yanked the reins again.

Jessie started to get up but Henry pulled her back down. "Not yet. Wait until they're inside the trailer. Then we'll all make a run for the barn." They watched as the man pulled Dragon up the ramp. It seemed to take forever. Finally, Dragon disappeared into the trailer.

The children raced from the field to the barn. Inside, four horses stood tied near the door. "Lots-o'-Dots!" said Benny, hugging his horse.

"Not now." Henry pulled his little brother into one of the back stalls. The children huddled in a dark corner as the man walked into the barn. They held their breath as he untied a pretty red horse and led it out to the truck. A piece of paper was tacked to the stall wall. Someone had written a list of horses: *Palomino, quarter horse, gray Arabian, brown spotted pony.* "These are the horses he's stealing," said Henry. "We have to stop him."

Jessie jumped up. "I can slow him down!" She darted to the last three horses and untied their ropes. Then she slapped them on the rear. They bolted out of the barn.

The man on the truck saw the horses escaping. "Hey!" he yelled. He jumped off the truck, chasing them. "Hey!"

The children peeked out from the barn. The man ran one way, then the other. "Roy!" the man yelled. "Come help me!"

The children ducked back as the truck door swung open and the driver stepped down. He had bright red hair and wore a white baseball cap turned backwards.

"That's the man who brought back Honey and Bunny," said Benny. "He drove the trailer with the dinosaur stickers."

The man in the striped shirt captured one of the horses and led it back to the truck. "Help me catch the other two," he snarled.

"No way," said the red-haired man. He leaned against the truck, laughing. "My brother and I steal 'em and we pay you to take care of 'em. It's your job to load 'em into the truck."

"You and your brother are the sorriest horse thieves I ever did work for," said the man in the striped shirt, chasing the last two horses. He kept stopping to catch his breath. Benny stared at the driver's Adam's apple. It bobbed up and down, just like Slim's.

"He must be Slim's brother," said Benny. "Slim has black hair, but the hair on his arms is red."

"He disguises himself," Jessie said, "the way he disguises these horses."

The man finally captured a silver horse that had stopped to nibble fruit from a crab apple tree. Only Lots-o'-Dots was still loose.

"We have to *do* something," said Benny.

"I have an idea," said Henry. "Violet, you go around to the front of the truck. Talk to the driver."

The shy girl blinked. "What will I talk *about?*"

"Anything," said Henry. "Just make sure you stand facing the truck. He'll have to turn his back to it while he talks to you. That way he won't see us." Henry put his hands on Benny's shoulders. "I need you to go out in the field and call Lots-o'-Dots. He'll come to you. The man out there will try to chase you away. Stall him as long as you can."

"What about me?" said Jessie.

Henry smiled. "You'll come with me. It's our turn to steal some horses."

*   *   *

The children waited until the man in the striped shirt jumped off the truck and began chasing Lots-o'-Dots. "Now," said Henry.

Violet took a deep breath and walked around to the front of the truck. "Hello," she said. Her voice came out like a squeak.

The driver whirled around. "Where did you come from?"

"The city," she said. "Greenfield. In Connecticut. Of, course, *this* is Connecticut, too. But Greenfield is very far away. I'm a tourist. And, um, I'm interested in horses. And, um, I was wondering if you could tell me—um—something about horses and . . ." Violet kept talking and talking as fast as she could. She had no idea what she was going to say next until the words popped out of her mouth.

Meanwhile, Benny ran out to the pasture. The man in the striped shirt was trying to catch Lots-o'-Dots. But the little horse kept trotting away. The man's shirt was all sweaty. He ran slower and slower. "Come back here," he shouted. But Lots-o'-Dots didn't listen.

"Here, boy," called Benny. The little horse looked up. Benny waved. Lots-o'-Dots pranced over to him.

"Hey, kid," the man ran toward Benny, panting. "Gimme . . . that horse. You shouldn't . . . be out here," he gasped.

While the two younger children kept the men busy, Henry and Jessie dashed up the ramp into the truck. It was packed tight with horses. Their reins were hitched to poles on both sides of the truck. "Untie them," whispered Henry.

They quickly untied one horse after

another. Then Henry climbed on the pretty red horse and Jessie climbed on Dragon. The children made clicking sounds with their mouths. Slowly, they eased their horses down the ramp and all the others followed. The driver spun around at the sound of hooves banging down the ramp.

"Hey!" he yelled, running to the back of the truck.

"Stop!" yelled the man in the striped shirt.

But the horses didn't stop. They scattered in all directions.

"Oh, Henry, how will we catch them all?" cried Jessie.

"You kids!" yelled the men, running toward Benny and Violet. "Stop!"

Jessie watched in horror as the thieves closed in on the two young children.

Suddenly, a voice yelled, "Eeeeeee-haaaa!" The children looked up. "Eeeeeee-haaaa!" shouted Alyssa as her horse burst out of the hay field. The wrangler raced full speed, waving her red hat in the air, charging right at the men. The men turned and ran. Alyssa whirled her horse around and rode up to Benny. She reached down. "Grab my arm," she said. Benny grabbed hold and Alyssa swung him up onto the saddle behind her. Henry pulled Violet up behind him.

"We have to save the horses," cried Jessie.

"Round 'em up!" Alyssa commanded, galloping after the scattered horses.

"Eeeeeeee-haaaaa," they all yelled, chasing the horses away from the truck. "Eeeeeeee-haaaaa," not stopping until they rounded up every last horse and ran them back to the safety of the corral.

CHAPTER 10

S'more Fun

Cookie drove up as the children rode into the corral. They quickly told her about the horse thieves and they all ran inside to call the police. Slim sat at the office computer. He jumped up when they came in. "Just a little computer work," he said, quickly turning off the computer. He looked at the serious group. "What's going on?"

Henry picked up the phone, dialing. "I'm calling the police to arrest your horse-thieving brother and your friend."

Slim's face turned white. "My what!?"

"You stole horses," Jessie said "and you stole my camera."

"W-why would I do that?" His Adam's apple bobbed wildly.

"Because," Violet said, "your friend at the old barn saw us taking pictures of your horses. Our photos were proof that your 'rescue horses' were really stolen horses. You tried to get rid of the evidence by stealing Jessie's camera."

"Why, that's crazy talk," said Slim.

"No one saw the camera thief come into this office," said Violet. "Cookie told us you're in here all the time using the computer, so no one suspected you were the thief."

Henry hung up the phone. "The police are on their way," he said.

Slim lunged for the door. Suddenly, Bucky stepped into the doorway. His short wide body blocked Slim's escape. "I always thought you were a terrible vet," said Bucky.

"Any vet worth his salt would have known Dragon needed a special square-toed shoe. I was the one who spotted it. I had to tell you. Even then, you didn't know what I was talking about."

"You told Alyssa to keep Dragon in the west pasture until his leg healed," Jessie said. "His leg was fine. You just wanted to steal him. You used black shoe polish to cover the white dragon marking on his back. You're the one who dumped oats near the fence. When Dragon and the other horses came to eat the oats, you stole Dragon and took him to the old barn."

Sirens wailed in the distance. Soon, Slim and his friends were all on the way to jail.

*   *   *

The Aldens sat with the ranch hands cooking hot dogs over the campfire. Kurt had stacked a pile of wood to keep the small fire going. Benny dropped two hot dogs into the fire before he finally got one to stay on his stick.

"I'm so mad at myself," Kurt said. "I should have seen that Slim was a fake."

"You were too busy trying to get Alyssa fired," said Cookie. "You weren't paying attention to your work."

Kurt turned to Alyssa. "I'm real sorry about that," Kurt said. "I was just trying to help my friend get a job."

"You let Honey and Bunny go, didn't you?" said Henry. "Then you broke the fence, and put the tree branch there to make it look like it was an accident."

The cowboy hung his head, ashamed. "I thought losing a couple of horses would make Alyssa look bad. I had to make it look like she let them wander away from the pasture."

Bucky smiled. "Those two lazy bones didn't wander far. Slim's brother confessed that he saw them wandering along the fence. He was afraid that a couple of missing Dare to Dream horses might bring the police. And he sure didn't want the police sniffing around this ranch. Not with all the stolen horses they'd hidden in the old pasture. So he loaded Honey and Bunny into his trailer and brought them back."

Cookie narrowed her eyes at Kurt. "I should fire you right this minute," she said. "For all the trouble you've put Alyssa and the rest of us through."

"I'm all right," Alyssa said. She turned to Kurt. "I'm tougher than you think. And maybe a little smarter. Last night I went to the library to find that book Slim said he wrote, *How to Raise Dogs*. I wanted to read it today on my day off. The librarian couldn't find it anywhere. So, I drove here to ask Slim if I had the right title. I saw that big horse trailer sitting in the west pasture. Slim didn't tell me he had horses coming in or going out. So I went to check it out." She looked at the children. "When I saw your horses saddled up and wandering loose in the hay field, I knew something was wrong."

Kurt took off his hat and held it over his heart. "Cookie, Alyssa, I'm sorry for all the hurt I caused," he said, sadly. "But I would like a second chance."

"I don't know . . . " said Cookie.

"Don't be too hard on him," said Bucky. "We all make mistakes. At least his mistake was done out of friendship."

Benny squirted mustard on his hot dog. "Bucky, you said we all make mistakes. Did you make mistakes when you were my age?" he asked.

"Sure," said Bucky.

"Like what?" Benny asked.

Even in the light of the campfire, the children saw Bucky's face turn deep red. "Well," he said, "like when I was a boy, just a little older than you, I moved away from my best friend in the whole world. And I never once picked up a pen and paper to write her a letter. I never once told her . . . how much I missed her."

Cookie leaned forward, staring hard at Bucky's face. "Trevor?" she said. "Trevor Austin? Is that really and truly you?" The old man nodded. Cookie jumped up. "Why in tarnation didn't you say something?"

"I wasn't sure you'd remember me. I thought if I came here and volunteered, you'd get to like me. It's been fifty years. I never once wrote. I wasn't sure you'd want to see me."

"Want to see you!" She reached out and gave him a giant hug. "I've spent the last fifty years wondering what in the Sam Hill happened to you. Of course I want to see you! You're my best friend, always and forever." They hugged and hugged until Benny had to remind them it was time to make s'mores.

*   *   *

Later, as the fire cooled, Cookie sat next to Bucky, both of them glowing in the campfire's light. Henry put one last piece of chocolate on one last graham cracker and added one last marshmallow on top. "I think I figured out the mystery of the hearts carved into the maple tree and in Dragon's stall," said Henry, "the ones with *TA* and *LM* carved inside . . . Trevor is you, Bucky—Trevor Austin."

Bucky smiled shyly.

Henry went on. "And, Cookie, I know

your last name is Miller. But what is your real first name?"

Cookie tilted her head to one side, a secret smile on her lips. "Well, now," she said. "Folks have called me Cookie since I was knee high to a grasshopper. I'm afraid my real name is one mystery the Alden children are just going to have to leave unsolved."

And they did.